The

Itty-Bitty

Nitty-Gritty

Non-literary

Non-magazine

Publishing Company: Books on Demand, Copenhagen, Denmark

Print: Books on Demand, Norderstedt,Germany

ISBN 9788743027669

The Itty-Bitty Nitty-Gritty Non-Literary Non-Magazine

Poems, prose, short stories and other writings by

Henrik Neergaard

Publishing House BoD, Books-on-Demand

WOW! It's a BOOK!

Other books by Henrik Neergaard published by BoD
Publishing House

My nightly wanderings under shining stars and darken sky

The serpent and the forbidden fruit

It is

Rather

peculiar

with this white paper. Yes, Of course, I do not mean to say that the peculiarity is related to the fact that the paper is white, as one might think from a superficial point of view. Nevertheless, it is a fact that the paper I am writing is white and it cannot therefore be questioned or described in any well-founded way as incorrectly as attaching the adjective white to the noun paper, as has happened in the introductory sentence of this paragraph, which is at the same time the first sentence on this page.

Nevertheless, I am not fully aware of why I came up with the emphasis that the paper is white. It seems to me that this is not fully justified. Well, it is not very natural to describe the paper as white, when it can now be established with certainty that it is actually the colour it has, one might ask.

On the other, however, the opposite view can be just as rightly argued, namely that there is no particular reason to describe the paper as white simply because it is the colour it has, but that a further justification is required to highlight this very fact above all the other characteristics associated with this piece of paper.

Or, in other words, that a specific intent or purpose is required for this description. Here it might be a nearby assumption that the purpose was to give a description that tells us something about one of the other concepts that appears in the sentence, of course, first and foremost the most significant of these.

On the other hand, it must be admitted that the purpose could also simply be to follow a linguistic tradition of linking certain adjectives to some nouns, so often given the opportunity to do so. that could be with this linguistic act would be prohibitive work. Or at least a work that exceeds the scope of this manufacturing.

THE WHEELS SPIN IN THE NIGHT

Hear how the big wheels are
spinning in the night

They spin in the dark

While you can barely see them

Only hear their ancient squeak
and squeak

Their scratchy sounds cannot
be hidden

Do not think about lubrication

For these creaking wheels

To make them run easier

For they can only be lubricated
with the blood

From tormented animals

Or humans

Leave the wheels be

Leave them as they are

Let them squeak and squeak

Put aside your impatience

Leave the sledgehammer

Don't smash a lock

Or a cog

Or ten

Or a thousand

Because you don't know

What happens next

Whether the machine slows
down

Or whether it stops

Or whether it might speed up

And run away

And crushes you and your city

Leave the sledgehammer

For no one knows

The day's progress

And backflow

In these nights of ore and rust

These days of raw iron and
scrap

And no one knows more

What is what

Don't force the metal to solidify

Before it is cast

Leave it alone

As it is

These days of locks and keys

These busy days

Where thousands of locks

Opens and closes

Every second

These hectic days

Where keys get lost

Being stolen

Counterfeit

And imitated

Used to the contrary

Or forged about

Where keys become locks

And locks turn into keys

Which even the wise don't
understand

Leave the keys alone

Leave the locks locked

And let the keys be keys

Do not try to change them
around

Leave the machinery

Do not fall for the temptation

To tinker with it

Do not think you can adjust it

Do not give in to the illusion

That you know it works

It has so many

Secluded corners and byways

Not even the engineers

Know its construction

Not even they

Would know the codes needed

The codes to lock

What to lock

And what to unlock

What needs to be opened up

What needs to be closed down

Leave the machinery alone

Do not touch it too soon

In these days

Of shifting gears

And changing directions

Suddenly, it changes and turns

In choppy alternating current

Suddenly pulsating against

All previously known plans

Old rules suddenly extinct

Or turning into the opposite

Let the wheels run by
themselves

Keep it simple

Just drive through your city

Do your work

Earn some money

For your self and your family

Eat your food and enjoy your
wine

While the sun is shining

And people can smile and laugh

While they can still forget

While they can still remember

While they can still work

And love and feel happy and
feel sad

Enjoy the night

And the peace of sleep

Or your drinks at a party

Do what you want

While the night is still up

Still standing

Let it help you

Through these hours

Where it is unclear

What is beautiful

What is ugly

What is good or evil

And you do not know

Whether you are dreaming or
still awake

Hold on to what you deeply
believe in

Hold on to your well-known
habits

Business as usual

Do not rock the boat

Do not be afraid to appear like
a sleepwalker

But be prepared to wake up

Be prepared for the sunlight

When it breaks its way forward

For another pale and chilly
morning

And stops the party

Or your sleep

And your dreams

With cold, revealing light

You know it deep down in your
mind

You cannot dodge it

Once nighttime is over

And the hours of dreaming are
gone

You will have to go out in
another morning

With cool grey light

One of those mornings

Chained to the ground

And the fields

And the rocks

To the sand

To the sea

To the cities

To the forests

And to the world

As it was in its origins

Before it was created

Before it was shaped

To become what it is

It was neither a jar

Or a box

Or a container

But just a lump of clay

They say, looking so wise

They keep up appearances

They look calm and collected

Beyond any doubt

As if this fact cannot scare

anyone

And least of all themselves

As if it were just a joke

Some weird practical joke

That these mornings

And workdays, and evenings

Are chained to the clouds

And blowing in the wind

Just like anything else

You cannot hide away

In the green, green grass

Or in the darkest forest

Or in your good intentions

Or in the singing birds

In the morning

And you know it only too well

Do not waste too much time

With sadness or grief

Just go along on your road

Your route through the city

Go along and smile to your
colleagues

when you get there

Tell them a funny

and cheerful story

Make them smile and laugh

Help them if they need help

Try to get along

The dices are still in play

They are not anyway near the
outcome of the game

They have not finished being
thrown

Do not disturb their dance
With your distrust
and taunting laughter
Your oh-so-smart handgrips
or your clever theories
Do not trim your trees
In the middle of a storm

Turn on the music you love

Turn up the volume

and have a dance

Distract yourself from the
sound

Of the giant wheels turning

Do not listen

to the sound of the things

That are being crushed

And destroyed

When the millstones are turning

Try to learn the art

Of relaxing

Of meditating

Of making no response

In the middle of the storm

You will need it to endure

The crushing sounds of the millstones

But be alert and beware

The office clerk's breakfast

Robert enjoyed the beautiful morning weather. The previous days it had been raining. It didn't now. The sun had come forth and shone down on its world from a clear, blay sky that wasonly beautifully decorated with a few small white clouds that looked quite and utterly innocent.

Robert had now arrived at the small café where he used to eat his breakfast every day.

Except on weekends. He himself considered himself a distinguished morning man who didn't like to stay in bed after seven o'clock. But his wife preferred to sleep long, and at least didn't want to interrupt her beauty sleep early to get up and make him breakfast. And Robert once felt that the food tasted him considerably better when some others had prepared it, so he had it served in a completely ready-to-eat version. That was how he had always felt, and this attitude to life had not diminished as he approached the 55.

Now he had made it all the way to the café and stepped inside the small cozy room. Some might think it was just legally dark and obscure, especially when you came in from the clear morning sunshine out on the street. But for Robert it was very comfortable, and especially at this time of day.

He knew both the host couple and the three waitresses for a long time. The host and his wife were good at keeping on the waitresses once they had found some, which both they and the guests were really happy with.

Robert stood up at the counter and waited. There was Julia behind the counter right now. She was probably really his favorite there on the spot, but he didn't notice. She smiled as big and charming as she used to, and he unconcerned the same as he used to. Coffee, juice, soft-boiled egg, 4 half rolls, one with cheese, one with jam and two with rolling sausage. As well as a morning bitter and a piece of pastry to finish with.

As usual, she was quick and efficient to deal with what he wanted after he had settled into the usual table in the corner, where he had an overview of the whole café, so that he could entertain himself with enjoying the sight of all the small, quirky steps that often played out between the more or less half-sleepers while he took his time to enjoy his morning coffee and his breakfast and his morning newspaper. And where he could sit a little secluded in peace and quiet and take his little box with that green something forward and sip a little on the contents in a discreet way and without summoning attention.

He had reached the third half when something drew his attention. A loud, sounding laugh. It sounded exactly like Julia when she was in her most exuberant mood. But there was also something that sounded like a man's laughter. And a young man's voice. Immediately, he lifted his eyes from the newspaper. It couldn't possibly be what he thought it was. The irritating upstart who thought he was something and who was so preoccupied with himself and his own imaginary excellence, so that he completely ignored the natural superiority and greater knowledge of the older and more experienced employees.

Was he here, too? Yes, apparently he was. He was everywhere. And now he had invaded his breakfast place, too. And not only that, he stood and flirted shamelessly and uninhibitedly with the best looking and most charming of the waitresses. So violent and so blatant, that it could only be described as deeply embarrassing, and almost as something that could have been used as a prelude to an erotic film. It certainly wasn't much wrong, he thought.

It was not, of course, because they were actually hitting each other, not with their hands at least, but one could hardly help but imagine a continuation in that direction. It was too bad though! That they were not ashamed! Today, the young people today had no inhibitions at all! It was incredible that the cafe's owner allowed his employees to behave in this way without intervening. He didn't think that about her.

It almost seemed as if the two already knew each other. There was something about their tone, and the flirtatious and petty way in which they laughed and laughed and talked to each other.

It was, however, the worst thing he had been subjected to in a long time.

The rest of the breakfast hardly tasted him at all. Only because the cafe made it as good as they once did, it slipped down anyway.

But what was that? The one who was a student had now sat down at a table a while away with a buddy who apparently was also really good friends with Julia. And which she also willingly flirted with, the shameless tether. He really didn't expect that from her.

The student and his companion were now engaged in a lengthy conversation after Julia had finally left them to do her duties and work elsewhere in the cafe. It might seem like she was the one they were talking about,

or at least something like that. But they sat
so far away that he could only occasionally
pick up a few words of their conversation.
Was she the one they were discussing? It
was annoying that he couldn't hear it all. It
could be very interesting to hear how they
talked about her. The individual fragments
he could intercept gave him no answer at all
to any of what he was wondering. and only
made him even more frustrated because it
piqued his curiosity.

He suddenly saw that those who had sat at
the table next to the student and his
companion had stood up and had left. Now
he had the chance, he thought. Frantically,
he gathered his things together, placed them
on the tray, but of course dropped the empty
egg cup on the floor. However, he had it
picked up and was about to stand up to
conquer the vacant table when he saw that
there were some others who had pre-empted
him. It was three young craftsmen who sat
down at the table next to the student. All

the other tables nearby were busy. However, it was annoying.

Disappointed and resigned, he had to stay seated at the table he was sitting at. What kind of place had his good old breakfast café evolved into? What kind of world was the world that was now living in, he thought bitterly, before leaning back in his chair and noting that the coffee pot was also empty, now that he really needed something to strengthen himself. In a brooding voice, he summoned a waitress and misplaced a new jug of coffee and a double morning bitter. And then it wasn't even Julia who came, but the host's wife, a skinny, tight-lipter and more than middle-aged gimpe, who was the only one of the staff at the cafe. As he had a hard time, was the world going all the way out of the making?

POEM

No. 2

There are houses that are gray

There are men and women that must go

Across the streets so small and narrow

Where the worn-out pawing trebles

Under every step they take

While they are munching nuts

Exchanging hats

Or whatever they will want to do

If they only dare to it

There are umbrellas when it rains

There's sunshine when it stops

Or weather grey and gruesome

Or snowy weather in the wintertime

Or storms that steal your hat

And leave you with a cold

When you go out onto the streets

It's too bad

And it must be fixed

That hotdog pushing man

He is a pain in the ass

It's too bad

He does not sell ant beers

His wife will not let him

She is crooked old lady

And he is a sissy

An obedient husband

He does not have the guts

To argue with her

It's too bad

And that's the reason why

So many people

Have to wander off in need

From the hotdog man's hotdog stand

With a stomach full of hotdogs, sausages

Steak sandwiches or burgers

But without a trace of beer

In their stomach

Full of thirst and anger

And empty, run out of thoughts to think

It's too bad

That all those people they must go

Plagued of thirst

In the middle of this city desert

In a tiny square

With houses that are grey

And so especially in this rain

Without umbrellas

They are much too wet on the outside

And much too dry inside

It's too bad

And all those people

They are getting mad

And they scare a poor old woman

All because of the stupid hotdog man

It's too bad

That all those people have to go thirsty

Between those houses that are gray

And in such a sad and rainy weather

With no umbrellas

City roads

In the town where he grew up, you did not just go to a patisserie. Admittedly, there were as many as three patisseries. Or at least bakery shops with serving. Especially in one of them (what was the most expensive) they had some delicious, delicious, delicious cakes that you had rarely tasted like, at least not there in the city.

Still, it wasn't as simple (as you might have thought) that you just went to the pastry shop, pushed the door open and stepped inside and went and sat down at one of the small round café tables with neat white freshly ironed tablecloths and ordered a cake and a cup of tea (or coffee or hot chocolate, for that they served too). There was undoubtedly a preponderance of tea drinkers at the patisserie. But especially if you were a healthy boy, or wanted to be, you didn't just go to a patisserie. No matter how delicious the cakes were, it could give you a bad reputation if you were seen in a place like that. And you were almost always seen. That's just the way it was.

You didn't just walk to the other end of town, or just the other half. This was true regardless of whether one belonged (that is to say lived) in one part or the other of the city. No matter in which part you came from, the easiest part was to take a shortcut through the large, beautiful park with its large lawns, decorative shrubets and large shady trees. And the lavish and always very manicured flower beds, not forgetting.

The park had the most central location in the whole city. It was right in the middle of town like a giant butter hole. It largely divided the city into two. The explanation for this was simple enough once you had been told. Originally (that is, in the real old days, many hundreds of years ago), there had been a semi-large provincial town on one side of the park. On the south side. What once was once more than a hundred years ago would probably have been called a market town. And only that. Neither park nor any town on the other side of where the park now lay. That's how it had been for centuries.

The market town was old and venerable and dates back to the Middle Ages. Or maybe longer still. At least it was really old. And very respectable. Back in the Middle Ages it had been quite a big city, after that time. Back then, it had had both churches and monasteries. As many as five monasteries had been there. Three monasteries and two nun monasteries. And as many as seven churches. It was back in the Catholic era before the Reformation, because then the monasteries were abolished. And also some of the churches. The king had nationalized all the monastic estates. So now the church had become poor and had to save where you could. As a result, three of the city's churches were demolished. So now only four of the old medieval churches remained.

But back then, before the Reformation, the many churches and monasteries had given the city some significance and a great reputation throughout the surrounding area. This long historical past was still reflected in the central parts of the city with the narrow, crooked streets of the picturesque old buildings, which, in the interests of fate and due to the city's later poverty and lack of momentum, remain largely unchanged until our days, in each in the exterior.

When the city finally began to gain some momentum, some 100 years ago, after centuries of thorny sleep, there was a circle of influential and culture-bearing but also rather conservative-minded citizens who were in power on the city council and, moreover, set the agenda for what was going on in the city. This group of solid citizens decided even then that the old, venerable buildings in the oldest district should not be demolished in favour of the new construction of more modern houses, as happened in many other cities at the time. Instead, they had to be preserved and refurbished.

There was probably also a connection with the geography of the city and its location in the countryside. The fact was that, just outside the city, there was a large open area which, particularly on the east side of the old market town, spread over quite a large area. This area consisted partly of lush but now dewatered meadows, and partly of the ancient exaggeration, which in previous centuries had been used for grazing the livestock of the peasants in the village that was on the other side of the overpass, i.e. further away from the market town.

But by the end of the 1700s, these vast areas had come to belong to the large estate, whose impressive, castle-like main building was about 15 km

from the old market town. The county
as it was called. From there, the area
had been run for many years as part of
the estate's agriculture. But the old
widowed countenance, who died
childless in 1929, almost 100 years old,
had decided in his will that this whole
area should be laid out as a public
park for the people of the market
town. This was much to the regret of
the slightly distant relatives who were
her sole heirs and who for decades had
looked forward to earning rushing
with money to turn the area into new
construction of various kinds, now
that more time was emerging in the
city's business and entire development
and therefore needed to build both
housing offices and factories.

But the greedy heirs all got a long nose. And the city got a park that would have been worthy of an international metropolis.

As already mentioned, east of the park was an old village. It was a small poor village with old, dilapidated half-timbered houses. It was there that the market town's manufacturers chose to lay down their workshops, factories, warehouses and office buildings. And it was also here, bypassing the old peasant town, that in theearly 1900s and subsequent decades entire neighbourhoods were built with cheap rental barracks for the workers and small rubbed townhouses for white-collar workers.

To the west of the park was the old market town with its well-preserved medieval streets, which tourists today are so excited about. And bypassing the narrow streets of the old market town, on its western outskirts, the city's more affluent citizens, manufacturers, shopkeepers, and senior officials and officials had then built their large, beautiful and elegant villas.

Such was the basic structure of the city. And in that way, the city was geographically divided in two. Although for many years, and indeed almost always, it had been regarded as one city of joint city councils and authorities, and was also officially there, many of us saw it as a kind of double city. A town somewhat like a pair of twins. And just as in human twin pairs there is often a dominant twin who decides most of anything, while the other is more meek and restrained, so was it here too.

Therefore, it was not simply self-evident to go all the way through the large park and into the other part of the city if there was no good justification for it. Nor were any guards or other law enforcement officers stopping one. But there could almost as well have been.

The three patisseries were all located in the fine old part of town, and the patisseries were considered somewhat distinguished and exclusive. They had a special status in the city. They were

up to a high standard. They were
considered upper-class. Too much
upper-class for common people. And
especially for boys. It would have
been like that in the past. All three
pastry shops were old and traditional.
They all had at least 100 years on
their backs.

Theodor Emanuel Rasmussen, about
whom this autobiography is supposed
to be, on which I am merely some kind
of ghost writer, was born and raised in
the other end of town. On the wrong
side of town, you may put it. That is,
the poor part of the city where the
working-class neighbourhoods were
located. Specifically, in some rather
run-down rental barracks well east of

the park. Way out by the freeway. Same as me, by the way, I grew up in the very same settlement, only a few blocks away.

After all, the park itself was a large gap between the two parts of the city. Some called the park a no-man's land, but it was only a few. Most people back then knew only too well to speak softly and not to question things as they were. There was an unwritten (but nonetheless very present) rule that, if you could not say something positive about someone (or something), then it was much better (or even considerably wiser) to keep your mouth shut. And it went far beyond the modern trend of positive thinking, I can assure you of that.

Even the large, purely physical area of the park was not ventured too far into, unless you had some kind of legal errand, at least not by us from the eastern end of the city. Of course, no one officially used the term legal errand, but that is how it was perceived, and how it worked in practice. On the whole, there were many more unwritten rules that we all knew by heart, and which, for the most part, we did not see at all as rules that anyone had adopted or laid down, but rather as some local laws of nature. Something that it made just as little sense to discuss or question, as the darkness of night, or the cold weather during winter, or getting wet when it rains.

That's how I believe it was for all of us who grew up there. Presumably it was somewhat pronounced for us from the east side, but actually I think it applied to everyone. And for the adults too, probably on a much greater scale than we as children imagined.

Finally, there were things that had to be looked after all the time. Larger and smaller duties of different kinds. School was the largest and most concrete and the most time-consuming of all the duties, but there were many other things that also had to be looked after. Such as homework, washing dishes, morning gymnastics, running errands, fixed return times and many others, sometimes also some that are not due to be mentioned here and which, in the clarity of looking back, seem much more meaningless now than they did at the time.

This is, of course, only his own and therefore subjective assessment. My old friend Theodor Emanuel has stressed this to me several times. But anyway, he explicitly asked me not to mention them in detail, possibly for the sake of readers, possibly because he did not want to exhibit his own sissy behavior.

Since I am simply out to portray his upbringing and other lives as it was, and almost to do him a favour, I have no reason to present everything I came across during my research. Suffice it to say that part of it is about

the unwritten rules of effective
bullying that they were practiced at
the time, both by the teachers towards
the pupils and among the pupils
among themselves. His own role in
this, on the other hand, there is no
reason to go into.

Such are the conditions for a ghost
writer – which is my job as an
experienced journalist. With my
professional background and based on
our joint upbringing and schooling in
the same part of town, I have
accepted to help him writing his
autobiography on the occasion of his
impending 60th birthday, which,
incidentally, almost coincides with the
25th anniversary of the big company
he has built up from scratch.

These are the terms, as it is called. Or to become more specific: at least the terms that I had solemnly signed when I signed the contract with him, when he (after a great deal of persuasion and a good dinner at the city's most expensive restaurant with up to several bottles of wine of really high quality and associated price level, obviously on my bill) finally hired me to write down his autobiography in a more professional and readable version than he himself was capable of producing.

Let me just add, for the sake of order, that almost everything in this autobiography about Theodor Emanuel Rasmussen, which I am helping him write, is based on the things that he himself has personally told me. Of course, supplemented by the source material from other side and the research that I myself have had to provide in order to give a complete and correct picture of everything. But i guess that goes without saying. It is not so easy to be a ghost writer - as outsiders might be led to believe, if you know about it only from the media.

But let us get back to the narrative itself. It was this thing with these fine old patisseries, which it was not possible to gain access to in practice, especially if one came from the east side of the city, where most people lived. For some reason, he felt strongly attracted both to the park and to the pastry shop (the finest and most expensive of them), although both were forbidden territory for him. Or at least virtually prohibited. If not in any written paragraphs or ingerated verbal rules, then in practice – and he was well aware of this. But it was as if, instead of keeping him away from these places, this fact, rather whetted his appetite for them quite a lot.

And this was even to such an extent that it sometimes (or indeed quite often) even went beyond his fulfillment of his everyday duties, as they were once defined by parents, teachers, school principals and other adults (but not necessarily by himself, my research shows, even more than I remember it from our shared school days). It must be remembered that a lot of things were going on in a completely different way than later on. But that was not even the worst thing about it.

For those who do not know our city, where both he and I grew up and for many years were classmates, it may be obvious to underestimate the ingenious and intricate décor of the city, which at the time did not occur to us in plain text. To this extent it seemed to us self-evident that this was just the way it was and that these were the natural conditions that everyone had to adapt to. We simply assumed that it was probably such a city (as a general concept, that is, all cities) necessarily had to be designed to function reasonably as a city.

It may seem naïve, and out of step with conditions elsewhere. But that is the way it was for us back then. Beyond question. We did not know any other cities than our own, and if we accidentally did, not in nearly the same thorough way, but at most as a short and superficial description that we had read about in the newspaper or became acquainted with the geography book. It happened occasionally that some of us visited a grandmother or an uncle or an aunt in another town or county, but it did not provide any real basis for comparison at all, since in these cases it was a short holiday with all the differences it can give from daily life.

Nevertheless, I still do not believe that our city was the only city that was decorated that way, or a similar way that was just as much like a maze. For it was probably precisely the key word if one had to briefly describe the overall structure and the whole mentality of the city, and the atmosphere that characterized the city and the people it housed.

Some of the city's streets were straight, others were crooked. The last ones were outnumbered. Often, a street you did not know showed that it was in a completely different place from the direction you had been expecting when it was turned. I read an article by a professor who claimed that it was probably just designed to make the experience all the greater, and thereby develop a special kind of discernment of the city's inhabitants. I think it's in full seriousness. It was a Professor K. K. Klausen from the University in a major Central German city, whom I interviewed a few years ago in connection with a series of articles on architectural theories, which I wrote for the newspaper I was employed at at the time before I was fired by the new editor-in-chief on a totally unfair basis. He, of course, formulated it in more form-complete and less sharp-cut statements than I would like to use space here to reproduce, and of course garnished with the usual professorial reservations, but there can hardly be any doubt that that was his point. Particularly interested can be referred to his later published thesis, "Untersuchungen zur Aufklärung der labyrintische Mittelalterstadtbau und seine politische Oekonomie, Verteidigung und Funktion."

But this intricate design was far from the only notable thing about these streets. Yes, basically not only the streets, but also the numerous small alleys and smokes and narrow paths that intersected especially the old western town, but also, to a large extent, the industrial area to the east. It was perhaps even a legitimate lyrical addition to call it an industrial area as such. In addition to the really

larger and smaller factories, it
consisted for a very large part of
countless small workshops, sheds,
outbuildings, warehouses, warehouses,
warehouses and the like, and most of
it had grown at the best of its kind,
without any organized urban planning
in the happy decades, when the only
sparsely tethered forces of the liberal
entrepreneurial spirit of chaos helped
to fully burn under the city's economic
prosperity and growth. The result had
also been that this, newer part of the
city almost surprisingly lived up to
the same unspoken ideal of an urban
structure inspired by spider webs and
labyrinthine puzzles as the oldest
parts of the old medieval town, also in
terms of purely physical design.

But beyond this there was another
curiousness which I think it is
necessary to mention. Namely, the
fact that most of the streets (and also
most of the smaller alleys, cigarettes,
paths and shortcuts etc.) apparently
coated with a thin layer of invisible
shards of glass, which one risked
cutting your shoes to pieces, if one
wanted to go from one place in the
city to another in an overly quick and
ill-thought-out way. And especially if
they were longer stretches that might
even lead into foreign districts,
because both the old and the newer
part of the city were of course also
divided and subdivided into a number
of smaller districts, which in the daily
way preferably had little to do with
each other.

Therefore, many of the city's inhabitants stayed inside their homes when they were not forced to move outside because, for example, they were going to work or school, or had other legal errands. In any case, it was common to stick to your own street, or your own small neighbourhood, where one had gradually acquired a certain sense of the local invisible glass shards. This, on the other hand, meant that the happy duties of family life were cultivated in rich measure, for the simple reason that there was little else to do once the other duties were over. That was before the time of both television and the Internet. This even took place to such an extent that it impressive many of the then quite few tourists who, after all, visited the city already at the time.

In recent years, the number of tourists arriving has grown quite considerably and is now one of the city's major sources of income. It's almost become a bit of a tourist magnet. Especially of course the old town centre with its narrow, crooked, labyrinthine streets and well-preserved old houses have become incredibly popular with tourists. And the four beautiful old churches and the old Gothic town hall and the other buildings back from the Middle Ages. In particular, there are certain specialised sub-segments of relatively wealthy and particularly historically and culturally interested tourists who are able to put quite a lot of money into the city if they want.

In the tourist brochures, the city is often described as an even living museum of a rarely seen design. But I think it is just something they have come up with at the tourist office because there's not much else they can advertise.

So that was the framework under which Theodor Emanuel Rasmussen grew up, but it is probably now the time to tell a little more about him as a person. Admittedly, he has already been mentioned (a little) but we better do it properly, when he is the one who is supposed to be the main character of this writing. Therefore, let us start by mentioning his name. Admittedly, it probably will not tell readers anything unless they happen to have been born and raised in the very same city as he and I (and I hope not).

His full name is: Theodor Emanuel Rasmussen, it is a fact. That is the name that his parents have chosen to give him as a christening gift for inscrutable reasons. I even have the impression that he himself was actually quite proud of that name. I am sure it has something to do with some family relationships. At least he was named after both of his grandparents.

One, Theodor Thomsen, was his maternal grandfather, and the other, Emanuel Eriksen, was his grandfather. At least according to the records in the church book, which, from experience, do not always contain the full truth about paternity for the children in a marriage, but which, after all, are, after all, supposed to do so for the most part.

One will probably immediately wonder why he bears a different surname from his grandfather (or the man who is at least listed in the church book as his grandfather), but according to several people I have spoken to, there is a perfectly logical and reasonable explanation for that (of course there is!), although it is not necessary to mention it here in this context.

More importantly, both Theodor Thomsen and Emanuel Eriksen were well-known and much-publicized people in this town, but unfortunately not always just for good. It should be added, however, that this was not solely due to their own greed, arriving morals and very poor situational awareness, but at least as much to the city's two leading gossip, who even claimed to have been secret mistresses with both of them in turn until they were wrecked in the most rude and degrading way.

On the other hand, they had subsequently found a very rewarding gossip object. Or rather, two very rewarding gossip articles, which they could even very often link together in a way that made the stories even better, and even at the same time in a way that, in many people's ears, sounded quite believable. After all, it had gradually become their metier, and they were adept at it.

Oh, what delight, they thought, the gossip, when they found out that the descendants of these two men, that is, Theodor Emanuel's parents, were getting married (with all their family baggage) – and especially when they found that his mother was already in the solemn marriage in the church so heavily pregnant that the wedding dress was about to burst. Back then, that in itself was more than enough to provoke a really solid round of outrage in ordinary people.

Part of the city gossip would know that the wedding took place only about a month and a half before the date his mother had the term to let little Theodor Emanuel arrive in this world and this small market town far out in the province, some would say, outside the law of the land and right. Some sources will reduce this to one month, others to three weeks or even 14 days. Yes, the most malevolent part of the gossip meant that it was only a little week's time, specifically five days (a few days say three days), adding that it was only because she had passed over the time of her imminent birth that she had even managed to get to church and be formally married to her future husband (who many believe was actually the child's father) before she had to go to the maternity clinic to bring little Theodor to the world.

However, my studies show, first of all, that there was far from agreement on this point. Some of my sources thus claim that she (i.e. his mother) started to contract her veer during the wedding dinner and had to be taken to the maternity clinic in haste. But there were also others who claimed that this was a gross misrepresentation of the course of events and that this could not possibly be the correct explanation. They could tell that she had already started moaning in a way while in the car from the church and to the function rooms where the wedding dinner was to take place, in a way that could only be due to advanced contractions, so that the car had to be quickly diverted to the maternity clinic, so the wedding dinner had to take place without the bride's presence, because she was inherently preoccupied with something far more important.

However, I also came across a third view which, with outrage, rejected both of these two explanations as pure nonsense. I quickly found that this view had quite a lot of followers, so it appeared to be the most widely used and popular description of how it had happened. The supporters of this theory adamantly claimed that the water had gone already while she was inside the church in front of the altar

and had not yet managed to answer
either yes or no to the priest's most
crucial question, but instead with the
water splashing down on the floor had
rushed out into the cemetery and
about behind the nearest bush where
she had then given birth to her child,
i.e. Theodor, on a small piece of lawn,
without even reaching the maternity
clinic. According to this description, it
must have been an exceptionally light
birth, with the baby almost slipping
out of her like a prun. At least that is
how I have heard it described by
several who claim to know the truth
about it.

It is also a fact that the small piece of
lawn in question at the back of a large
and lush bush in the cemetery to this

day is sometimes referred to by some elderly inhabitants of the city as "Theodor's lawn".

It is also reported that the bride's slightly intoxicated uncle had immediately shouted up inside the church when the birth had become known and by a church singer who had slept over her and had only now met at work had been whispered to one of the back-seated churchgoers, and from there as an ever-increasing whisper had spread up through the church from chair row to row of chairs. When it reached the intoxicated uncle, who, to the priest's great chagrin, had sat on one of the front benches, he cried out even more than before and demanded, in an almost threatening tone, that the child should be immediately carried into the church after being freed from the umbilical cord, so that one could get the child's face over immediately, now that the members of the two families had been drummed together with some difficulty.

This caused renewed unease both among the wedding guests, who had been seated on the church benches to obey the priest's repeated calls to remain calm, and because they did not know what else to do, and also with the by now rather angry and desperate priest.

However, this loud suggestion from the drunken uncle was immediately rejected by the priest in a rather indignant tone, repeating that christenings should be ordered from the choir clerk of the church office during his opening hours at least one week before the desired time of baptism. The drunken uncle was also not supported by the rest of the wedding guests, and when he fell asleep on the church bench shortly afterwards, the congregation calmed down again.

So much about the results of my research, which I am presenting here as soberly and objectively as possible. It can be argued with some court that the case could probably be settled fairly quickly and simply by contacting the church office and posting in the church books, or, alternatively, by studying Theodor Emanuel's birth certificate and his parents' marriage certificate. When I have chosen to refrain from this easy solution, it is purely because I prefer to rely on Theodor Emanuel Rasmussen's own statement in this area.

He has repeatedly stated to me that all these explanations are completely untrustworthy and arise only from malicious and overly fanciful gossip stories. After which he insists with great determination that there was at least seven months interval between his parents' wedding and his own birth. Note that he uses the term "least". (Later, moreover, he has extended to the nine-and-a-half month).) That is why I will do the same and endorse his conviction for the proper context of the cases, without showing him unnecessary mistrust or asking undue questions, but merely reproducing his own description of this for him as precisely and carefully as possible. (It is also, incidentally, one of those terms of the contract I had to sign to have him entrust me with the task of rencricting this his uncooked autobiography — obviously on the basis of his own slightly scattered notes, which hardly exceed a dozen sheets of large clumsy handwriting, and were therefore far from sufficient to constitute an entire book, which was of course he was in charge.)

Springtime Poets

The night stands black and
massive

The rain is falling in my
town

It falls on streets and
roads

On the roofs of the
houses

On lawns and shrubs

On flowers and sprouts
and trees

Washes the dust away

The streets are wet

With falling rain

Everyone stays inside

Waiting for the sun

And the heat

Nostalgia
Pages

Believe it or not, but it's 26.
Of December. We are very
unlikely to be serious. Now
we've come to something with a
flip button on the computers
instead of that old-fashioned
mouse from the 1900-and-
white cabbage that we're still

grappling with, so we get mouse arm and carpal tunnel syndrome

Now it was time to get a little more to eat and drink. We ordered a read of the caf é 's best sandwiches and some little half-expensive beers. It's only Christmas once a year. And by the way, it was Martin who was going to give this round.

We had only just finished swallowing the food when Martin was there again, i.e. with a new topic of discussion. A concrete proposal, in fact, it was. But now we had finally moved beyond the self-driving biler.nu it was something about computers. It turned out he had been on a long trip around the internet last night. And he had grown so tired of sitting up and down on those different sides

with the mouse and those scrolling shafts. So
he had come up with a much better way.

He wanted there to be a flip button on the
keyboard.

A Browser Button.

That's what he called it. So when you press it,
it switches to the next screen. So you can
browse through the content of a website, just
like when you browse a book. Instead of
having to sit and grease with the mouse all
the time. Or on that pressure-sensitive plate
on the laptops. It would be much easier and
faster, he said. Then you don't get the mouse
arm from having to sit and fencing with that
mouse and hitting it exactly with it in a very
small field.

But then I suppose it had to be built in a
different way, that is, the various sites on the
Internet, i.e. Paul. Yes, of course, martin said,
then it should be divided into screenshots.
That just matched what can be displayed on

the screen at once, without having to sit and scratch with the mouse. Like the pages of a book. But there may well be a subject that goes over multiple screens, like a chapter that fills many pages in a book. Then all the screens had to be numbered with page numbers, and at the front there should be a table of contents with the page numbers on each section. Then it would be much easier to find what you are looking for, rather than having to find your way through that branch or tree structure, where you often have to sit and guess on which subtopic it is located. The wooden structure from which it branches is such a real engineering thing that probably seems logical to those who construct it and even know all the content in advance. It is just not very practical for the ordinary people who need it.

But now he already came up with an addition. In reality, there should probably be three flip buttons. And they should be on the keyboard. One flip button must flip one page forward,

the other must flip a page backwards, and the
third must be one where you type the page
number into the numeric keypad, and press
flip button No. 3, and pling, then you get to
the side right away. It would be much easier
and faster than the current system, he said.
He sounded really excited about his idea.

There should surely not be much to say about
those Belgian trappist beers, but
apparently there was anyway

Even worse, it got worse when someone discovered that some of Malene's beers had been brewed at one of the trappist breweries in Belgium, and immediately roared it all over the place. Which made a witty dog roar back that kind of thing he shouldn't talk about out loud when it was just a brewery run by those trappist monks. That was how the mood had become at the time, and it became even more so – when he threw himself into a longer explanation of what it is all about with such a trappist brewery.

And that it has nothing to do with the fact that the beer was brewed at an old monastery from before the elevator was invented, even if it actually is. But that's just not why it's called that, because it has nothing to do with stairs at all. Hay, hay. But that it is rather about those who visit such a monastery not being told anything about what it is about, except by listening to everything that is not being said. Which, I don't think, is quite true, because I don't think it's only among

themselves that the monks are not allowed to
talk.

But, of course, there were some who had to
embroider on it, now that the subject had
been set in motion. Someone immediately
pointed out the paradox that this very trappist
beer, which, according to tradition, had been
brewed in deep silence, could make people as
eloquent as this discussion was a clear
example of this.

Then there was another one, and
unfortunately it was myself who had become
so eloquent by the fantastically good beer
that I aired a very profound theory at the time
that that was precisely why. That all the
words that were not said in the monastery
during the brewing of the beer, like still lying
hidden in the beer, as a kind of resource one
could draw on, or rather got poured into it
when you drank the beer. Like if you put the
money in the bank instead of spending it right
away. And so in return can use them later.

What I saw myself in rich measure. That is,
those saved words in the beer. I didn't even
think my explanation was silly until now
afterwards.

There's nothing to do about it,
but here comes something even
more about those trappist beers
and why they taste so good,

but I refuse to believe that the explanation is right, it's probably just nonsense from a drunk person at a Christmas party, so don't believe it. I might have gotten a little more sober, so I don't think that kind of thing is funny at all. I'm fucking sitting here writing it down while I still remember it, even though I should be sleeping it off.

But it was still full swing at that Christmas party. It pulled out, as things like it very often do. And as is probably the point.

They were still shouting and screaming at each other. So Bodil and Malene, sometimes everything else. They each had their own team of supporters who backed them, and now it was everything else they were arguing about. After all, they had already been through all the arguments several times, so it started to become a little monotonous. But then Bodil suddenly came back on the field with something more botched trappist mumbo-junbo and began a long story about it to turn a little more sympathy on to his side.

The story went that she had once heard of such a classic trappist brewery in the old days, when there was such a young monk, there was a kind of apprentice who had to look at how it all went with that beer brewing, so that he could learn for himself, and one day the old monk, who is a real professional brewer monk, has taken the lid off the big brew boiler to load some hops and some malt into it. He's turned around to take a sack of hops that's behind him. While he is fumbling to get a good grip on the hop bag, a large German shepherd comes running in through the door out to the open air, which is open due to the summer heat. In front of the dog runs a poor cat, which the dog is chasing across through the brewing hall. To get away from the dog, the cat takes a long leap over the open-faced brewing boiler, but it missteps its plunge and falls into the brewing boiler instead, and drowns instantly.

Meanwhile, the dog drowns out everything with its furious barking before running out of the brewing hall through the door at the opposite end, which is also open. The brewmaster has meanwhile got a good take on

the hop bag and has had the cord loosened,
which tied it together at the top. He just gets
to see the dog as it's on its way out as he
turns to the brewer again and starts pouring
all the hops from the big sack into it. He
clearly has no idea about the cat, which is at
the bottom of the brewing boiler and is
quickly completely covered in the hops.

The young apprentice monk does, in return.
He's seen it all, but now he has a problem. He
would of course like to make the brewmaster
aware of the cat in the boiler. But because
they're both trappist monks who have to live
in silence, he can't say anything about it.
Because then he would be violating trappist
rules. He is a pious monk who would like to
do it all by the book, so of course he will not
violate such a basic rule. And he is young and
very keen to be perfect as a monk. Then
sometimes he might interpret the rules extra
squarely.

Instead, he tries to make some gestures with his hands to mimic

A cat that comes running and jumps into the brewing circle, but the brewmaster doesn't understand his strange gestures and just shakes the head of the silly kid. So he still doesn't notice about the cat.

The brewmaster just continues his work of pouring in the other ingredients, and then he sets the brewing process in motion exactly as he usually does. So that means that the poor dead cat is being brewed in the portion of beer that has just been started in the brewing boiler.

Bodil smiled bell shocked and looked over the congregation for a moment before continuing.

Do you see what I mean? She said. I just don't want to drink this kind of beer with dead cats in it. she exclaimed and trashed, so it was clear to everyone that she had at least taken plenty of the other beer.

She apparently thought that she had thus demuted Malene's fancy foreign specialty beer, and at the same time had provided some sort of justification for her own more boring beer purchases, and that she had thus won the discussion about it with a kind of backhand fine.

She laughed about it herself, but that was nonsense. It was just a flat and stupid joke. It wasn't even really funny. She made herself funny at their expense. I mean, on the trappists. Those beer-brewing monks who couldn't even retraize against it without violating their own rules, as someone immediately mentioned. If they had heard Bodil's nonsense, what fortunately they couldn't.

I don't think that's the real thing. They certainly have some method to draw attention to something like that without having to open their mouths to say something about it. It was simply below the low. I tried to explain that to Bodil, too.

Maybe that's exactly what's the manufacturing secret, she said. Perhaps it's the core of their secret recipe that makes it so unique, she said, and cheered as she looked around for more applause, and the garbage grinned, so that the loose roof tiles at the neighboring house shook. Strangely, it made the happiness of an incredible number of people who cheered and clapped as if she were the queen of the party and the story of the dead cats in the beer was one of the evening's highlights.

Christmas lunch is still going on, and its philosophical heights have probably reached a new low, for now there's a long talk about those trappist monks who probably don't have such a Christmas party like this one.

Bodil, of course, basked in the rush of enthusiasm. However, soon got into gear when a middle-aged accountant began to explain something about how he thought it was going to such a place.

She was deeply unhappy about that, and therefore tried to capture the course again by shouting out at the congregation if anyone knew if those trappist monks had to send text messages to each other.

But no one knew, and the accountant quickly took the floor again and went on to say that they probably do not use mobile phones and computers in such a place, because it all takes place according to centuries-old methods and some special old recipes with hundreds of years on the back, and that is probably why the beer gets that particular aroma. It would not make sense if they had mobile phones when they are not allowed to talk to each other, and even with text messages they can have long conversations with each other, so that would be pure cheating, he said.

But on the other hand, he continued his long and very loud lecture about it, then they have probably developed their own methods of dealing with such things as the one with the cat in full silence. They've been brewing that beer for centuries, so they've probably found a solution to it, too. Maybe they have such an old mechanical apparatus sitting on the wall inside the brewing hall, back from the old days. One of those things where you just have to pull a handle and then there's a metal sign that says. "Have you remembered to put yeast in?" or "Remember to use the right type of malt" and then, of course, also one that says, "Be careful! A cat has been put in the brewing circle!""

I think he thought it was funny himself. But not many others thought so. I didn't think so either. For once, Bodil hit the nail on the head

when she said it was both corny and nonsense
and pure nonsense and also rather prejudiced.
Most people actually applauded that, and in
return, the bookkeeper applauded. But in the
end, things calmed down a little more, and for
a while it all seemed pretty normal. Bodil and
Malene didn't shout at each other quite so
much anymore either. It could be quite
entertaining sometimes. But now I think there
was only a few small frictions left between
them. Luckily, Malene woke me up before we
got home. Maybe she thought it was too
difficult if she was going to drag me down the
stairs.

She fell in love

with a library.

She kept it secret.

The problem is that Kirsten and Carl Peter have a slightly ambiguous relationship with his interest in football and all that. On the one hand, it is very nice for her that he has it to go up, so he is mostly at home on the sofa when he finishes the day's work in that job he has with a haulier. And that he invites friends to his house instead of running around to those out in the city.

It must give her some reassurance that he certainly doesn't make the wild displays. Although it can sometimes be going on when she is not at home, because she has to visit a friend, or if she goes to some evening school or something. She does that sometimes, but it is not often.

For the most part, she is home in the evenings and on weekends, so she can keep a little leash that he does not make too much of a. I think she almost thinks that all this kind of thing is a thing of the past for him. So I'm not going to cut shards by being too open-mouthed. There is no reason to put their marriage in jeopardy here just before the silver wedding, so we also miss that party, just as happened to Birgit and Søren a few years ago.

They split up with legal divorce and the whole moles just six months before their silver wedding because someone had been too open-mouthed about something one of them had been going on, or it was actually both of them. But there is no reason for that. It's just too silly.

But that's not really what I wanted to tell you. It is because in many ways she has a little different interests than those he cares about so much. But I guess that's the way it is.

But to give a rather important example, it has turned out that Kirsten suffers from an unhappy love of books and literature and things like that with philosophy and all the kind of thinking about life. And you know what that kind of thing can lead to. Even she herself has an unrealuminous urge to philosophise about things herself. She openly admits that. But maybe she's also a little influenced by her profession. Or quite a lot actually. People get that a lot. I know many examples of this. In fact, both good and bad, if I'm going to be a little objective.

But the fact of the matter is that she has been employed as a librarian at the local municipal library for many years. That was all very well, especially if she had stopped in time and retired, as planned, instead of continuing at half-time. That's where the chain jumped off. Actually, it was.

After all, she would have liked to have discussed what she was reading, and also her own excursions into the nooks and crannies of her mind, with her husband.

But that kind of didn't really interest Carl Peter. It was her great sadness that it was not possible. She's said that a lot. Many times. And precisely with the expression that it was her great sadness that she could not discuss things like that with Carl Peter. So I tend to think that's right enough.

That's probably why she definitely wanted to continue working half-time at the library. I think so. Then she could at least discuss it with her colleagues over there. For most of them, they were also very interested in books and all that. Although of course it also had a job they had to look after, so they couldn't just sit and discuss literature all day. Especially not after the recent cuts. But a little bit, maybe there might be time for some time.

But then it was that it happened. For a younger male librarian had just been hired

at the small local library where she was
employed. He was about the forty, I think,
at least a few years younger than her. And
he had a great interest in most of the
same writers and the same philosophers
with whom she was so preoccupied. It
could almost only go wrong. He was even
divorced. Newly divorced. Less than six
months ago.

So it went as it had to go. Before long,
they were complicated by long
philosophical and literary discussions
every day during the lunch break. Soon
they started to take a break in the local
caf é every afternoon after the end of the
work. Not to flirt or to cheat on anyone.
But only to continue their deep and
obviously very intense discussions about
books and literature and writers and
philosophy.

In fact, it went well for a long time. But
then it was that she got the ill-thought
that she would start working full-time
again. No doubt with the hidden agenda
and the secret purpose that there was
then the opportunity to spend even more
inspiring and intellectually stimulating
hours with his library heritage. And then,
of course, Carl Peter at home began to
wonder.

Because he had a good salary where he
worked, so there was plenty for both of
them with what he earned. He had already
told her more than once that she didn't
have to go to work because he earned
everything they needed. So she could
retire. They could do without her pay, he
said.

I do not know whether she directly argued
with women's rights to make their own
money and not to be dependent on a man

who could support them. But she certainly
didn't bow to his attempts to keep her at
home with her meat pots, frying pans and
his new dish.

Because that, of course, was Carl Peter's
real intention. Keeping her at home all the
time so she had a lot more time to go and
socialize with him and make more of the
household and the cooking, and all that
domestic stuff that he thought she was
starting to slop a little with here lately.
Whether it was right or not. But at least
that's where she said stop.

I think it almost made her more stubborn
and more determined to keep her job at
the library at almost any cost. She could
be like that sometimes. So she insisted.
And even taking some extra hours so she
actually got back up to full-time. Once
she had put something in her head, she
didn't give it up so easily again.

She wasn't completely lost in the back of a wagon, so she quickly turned her attention to the fact that it was a question of equality and women's politics and all the kind that used to put him a little to the wall. For all his other vices notwithstanding, however, he had finally followed so much over time that he did not like to be seen as an old-fashioned house tyrran and male chauvinist who oppressed women.

So Kirsten gave again with about the same coin one day when they sat at dinner. She suggested that he might as well stop working when she went full-time. Carl Peter was, after all, losing both a knife and a fork when she said it. what he was still entitled to. And why shouldn't the woman as well be the one who supported them both, as the man, she asked.

After all, he couldn't really give that back on without revealing himself as the oppressur of women; he was probably still a bit of deep down, despite all his attempts to keep up with the times and try to understand the trends that were moving in it. So then he was almost speechless.

So now she knew how to argue her case. So she went on to say that if he stopped working and let her make a profit, he could also take over all the household work and cleaning and cooking and laundry and all that stuff when he had to go home all day while she was at work anyway. That's when he became even more speechless. He never imagined that.

The idea that they could do without his masculine income was bad enough in itself. But the fact that he was also going to run around at home with an apron on and cook and clean and wash clothes while she was at work was just about to tear the rug away from under him. But as Kirsten sontilly put it: for decades she had been in charge of all these things while doing her job as a librarian, most of the years until recently even full-time.

So why wouldn't he be able to handle it when he was just walking at home all day, she asked. Then it wouldn't really be fair to swap a little bit about the roles now. Maybe he didn't think that sounded pretty reasonable? And had he ever had anything to complain about in connection with her housekeeping?

Carl Peter rushed to chop, but he probably should have let that go. He was stupid enough to mention it with her cooking in the first year of their marriage. Back then, she hadn't been very good at cooking. Pretty miserable, actually.

What he had complained about at the time
was that his mother had finally taken
action and taken his newlywed daughter-
in-law to school. Back then, Kirsten had
been much quieter and restrained than it
is now. And perhaps she had managed to
believe that it was a special Danish
tradition. Something that was quite
common in this country.

In any case, it had become that a young
newlywed couple would show up at their
mother-in-law's every weekday when they
came from work, and then the mother-in-
law otherwise started a quite scrimmed
cooking class for the son's newlywed wife,
with special emphasis on his son's
favorite foods and his penchant for thick
brown sauce. During a winter, Kirsten was
an almost perfect cook, at least on Carl
Peter's favorite dishes, but the humiliation
of being taken to school by the tough

mother-in-law who didn't think she did well enough for her son, she never forgot.

That is why it was, of course, also a major misstep on his part to bring this very matter forward. It really made him sound like a genuine old-fashioned male chauvinist and an ungrateful and demanding old-fashioned husband who almost regards his wife as some kind of slightly more upgraded maid or housekeeper.

It quickly dawned on him, almost immediately after the words had come out of his mouth. It was such an under-the-question argument that he alone had lost the discussion, and then he clapped like an oyster and let his wife work as much as she wanted, without further questions or comments. So she had the opportunity to enjoy the wonderful conversations about profound philosophical questions

and literary interpretations, along with her
increasingly dear library heritage- about
which Carl Peter fortunately knew nothing.

The occasion of it all

.... Was the simple one that I needed a shoelace. There was a shoelace broken in one of my shoes, as simple as that. But sometimes things are more complicated than you care. I don't really know why. That's just the way it is. Some say that it is usually oneself who makes things more complicated than they need to be. But I don't think so.

Well, that was that shoelace. Admittedly, it was also of a rather poor quality from the start. That, of course, was what was wrong. I had bought this weeks offer in some discount store and I had had

it lying in a drawer quite a long time before I put
it into use.

As it was, the problem actually started earlier,
namely when the previous shoelace broke.
Strangely enough, the laces on my left shoe always
break before it on the right shoe. I don't know
why,

But that's just the way it is. I don't know if anyone
else is the same way. It may have something to do
with whether you are right- or left-handed and
how much force you put into it when you tie the
right and left shoes, respectively.

So this was a left lacer that was broken only a few
months after I bought the shoes. While the right
laces were still completely intact. I think
it'sbadthat they don't make the laces properly so
that they can last.

But that's the way it is these days with so many
things, it's the pure slendrian with everything.

Everyone is just trying to score the box and get around easily at everything.

Well, when my shoelace broke, luckily I had an extra pair of shoelaces lying around. And it even actually fit the shoe. Same color, same length. Same thickness, too. It almost sounded like it was perfect, then. If you didn't know better. Of course, it wasn't that simple.

Hey!

This is Mom calling!

Hey, it's Mom.

I'll tell you what. That piece about Romeo and Juliet that you've been about in the studio. You could do that a little differently. Otherwise it will be so trivial if it always must stay the same.

What I'm thinking about, it's something like this: Romeo is some kind of a zombie,

or some kind of robot, or something. Or
no, it was something else I came up with.
If we're going to update it a little bit to
the present and stuff like that. So both
Romeo and Juliet are participants in such
a reality-show on TV. And then Romeo is
burned hot on Julie, but TV production
Don't want the two to get together.
Because he's looked after someone else
that Julie needs to pair with, because he
thinks they fit together better, and that it
fits better with the concept if it's Julie and
the other guy. And then he puts all sorts
of obstacles in the way of Romeo and
Juliet. Or maybe it's a female producer,
and it is all because she herself has
gotten hot on Romeo and wants him for
herself, and not on TV, but outside in the
real world, because she can see that he is
really in love with Juliet and the TV-
producer gets very jealous with Juliet.

And because of that, she designs her TV production to make a lot of trouble for Romeo and Juliet, so they do not get each other. So that is why she's creating all these difficulties that makes it so hard and troublesome for them, and then she tries to seduce him, but he doesn't respond to that because he only wants Julie. And the TV production runs both itself and the whole situation further and further out. But the more the TV producer tries to get in his pants, the more he focuses on Julie and only on Julie. Eventually, it becomes a pure power struggle between the TV producer and Romeo. The TV producer cannot just write Julie out of the show, because she's the star of the show and without her the viewership would drop dramatically. Then the TV producer gets one of the other men at the set to try and seduce Juliet. Of course, Juliet does not fall for that. Then the TV producer tries with another one of the male actors. And another. And yet another. Until she has tried all the male contestants. Some of them she has had to sleep with herself to persuade them to do it, because they are not very eager to go for Juliet. They think the TV producer is crazy and do not want to interfere with the way Shakespeare wrote the play. By mistake, the TV producer's hefty sex with the other men on the set is filmed and broadcasted. Or maybe it is rather because one of the technicians or photographers is mad at the TV producer because she's rejected his advances. So now he wants to take revenge on her by making sure that the sex scenes with her are included in the broadcasts. The TV station boss is considering firing the TV producer because it is a clear violation of the rules

of the broadcast. But the hefty sex scenes
with the TV producer make the declining
viewership rise enormously, so he does
not fire her after all. On the contrary, he
demands more sex scenes between the TV
producer and the male contestants, but
now they've had enough of her, so to get
the viewership back up he'll have to sleep
with her himself and make sure it's filmed
and joins the show. But one of the female
contestants has turned mad at the TV
company boss, because she was secretly
in love with him, but he rejected her in
order to sleep with the TV producer
instead, and now she is very angry about
that, so she swaps the TV boss's viagra
pills with some lime pellets, and then he
can't get it up, as it comes down to the
play and the film crew is already filming it
live. Viewers are, of course, furious about
this, and viewership plummets. Now the

TV boss has to come up with something in
a hurry if he doesn't want to lose his job
because of the dramatically declining
viewership. Fortunately, though, there is
still Romeo and Juliet, who have caused
so much trouble throughout the
broadcasts, but are nonetheless the most
popular with the viewers. But what he has
come up with now as a desperate attempt
at boosting the TV rankings, both Romeo
and Juliet think is totally crazy, and they
refuse to play the scenes he wants them
to play. Then the TV boss gets one of the
most underpaid of the technicians to put a
heavy sleeping remedy into the drinks to
be served to Romeo and Juliet at a
particularly wild party. But he's just an
unemployed person who's been sent to job
training at the tv station, and unlike most
people, he doesn't really bother with that
TV thing because he'd rather just sit at

home and smoke weed all the time. And
that very day he had smoked a lot of weed
before he was supposed to show up for
work. Then, by mistake, he gives Romeo's
drink to the TV boss and Juliet's drink to
an old cleaning maid, who has come to
clean in a completely different studio on
the tv station, but has had some difficulty
in finding her way around the place
because she has only just started to work
there. So instead of Romeo and Juliet, it is
the middle aged, overweight TV boss and
the old cleaning maid who fall into each
other's arms like distraught lovers who
can't get each other. Meanwhile, Romeo
and Juliet, who for once are not being
supervised by the TV producer, go out to
one of the toilets in the side wing and get
their first real bang on the tv station's
territory. They are so much in love, that
they forget about the security cameras in

all of the toilets, just like everywhere in the buildings. So, as a result, without their knowledge, their lovemaking is being filmed and broadcasted, even if it is in incredibly poor image quality. But the TV viewers love these scenes and viewership rises again. But then... ...

... hello, are you even listening? It's Mom trying to tell you something. Are you there... ...the sound from the TV is so loud I can't hear what you're saying? I just thought it was a great idea for one of your favorite TV shows. But it's the usual thing. You don't want to listen to any of Mom's advice, right?

My nightly wanderings under shining stars and darken sky

A novel

A man makes a bet at a damp Christmas get-together. He bet a female academic that he can write a book, even if he's not intellectual. And then he's going to have to write that book so as not to lose the bet. The book will contain a little of each about big and small experiences from his daily life. And also some thoughts and a little philosopher about things and phenomena in the world and in society. Not least the technical developments, where he and some friends are quite sceptical about the self-driving cars, because they like to sit behind the wheel and control their own car. Otherwise, it's just going to be a kind of public transport. I wonder, for example, that there is a great deal about a self-driving motorcycle? He himself says that the book is not autofiction – not ordinary autofiction in any case.

160 pages

ISBN 9788743016267